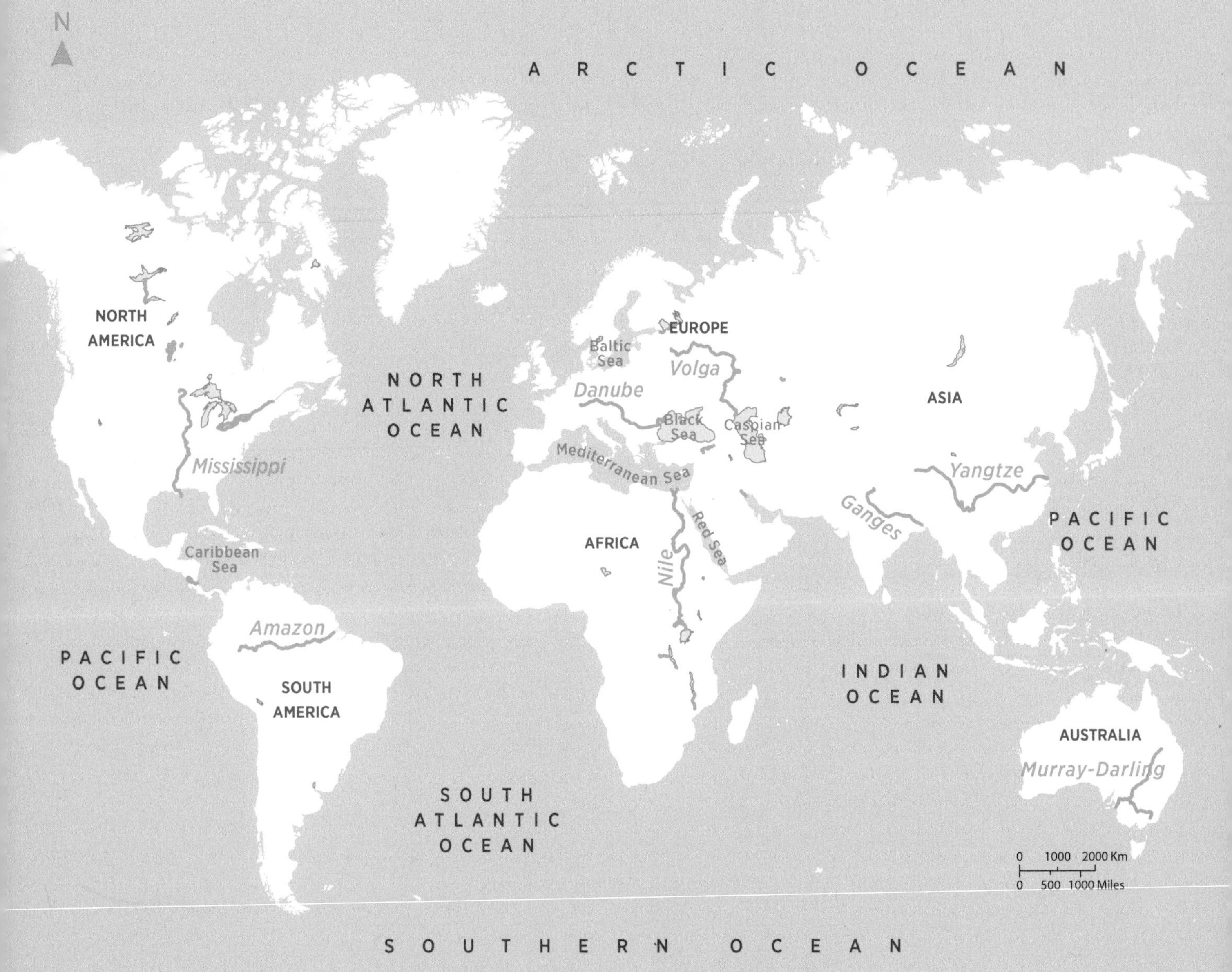
N
ARCTIC OCEAN
NORTH AMERICA
EUROPE
Baltic Sea
Volga
Danube
NORTH ATLANTIC OCEAN
ASIA
Black Sea
Caspian Sea
Mediterranean Sea
Mississippi
Yangtze
Ganges
Red Sea
PACIFIC OCEAN
AFRICA
Caribbean Sea
Nile
Amazon
PACIFIC OCEAN
SOUTH AMERICA
INDIAN OCEAN
AUSTRALIA
Murray-Darling
SOUTH ATLANTIC OCEAN
0 1000 2000 Km
0 500 1000 Miles
SOUTHERN OCEAN

Shiny

the Sea Star

Surfs the Seas and Finds

a Yangtze River Dragon

Cleopatra B. Alexander

Written and illustrated by
Cleopatra B. Alexander

Also by Cleopatra B. Alexander

Shiny the Sea Star Surfs the Seas and Finds
a Mississippi River Paddlewheel Boat

Shiny la Estrella de Mar, Surfea los Mares y Encuentra
un Dragón en el Río Yangtze

Shiny la Estrella de Mar, Surfea los Mares y Encuentra
un Barco a Vapor de Ruedas del Río Mississippi

Shiny the Sea Star
Surfs the Seas and finds
a Yangtze River Dragon

Written and illustrated by
Cleopatra B. Alexander

WaveRider Press
Evanston, IL

Cleopatra Bugelas Alexander

www.shinyseastar.com

First Edition
Designed by María Vélez

Library of Congress Control Number: 2017902933
ISBN: 978-0-9968666-0-6
eBook ISBN: 978-0-9968666-4-4
Printed in the United States of America
WaveRider Press
www.waveriderpress.com

For Nicholas and Elena
Love ya, Yiayia

Good Morning, Shiny,
said Shiny the Sea Star's Mom.
Have some cereal.

Good Morning, Mom.
I'll have some Kelp-O's, please.

Guess what, Shiny! I had a very
happy dream last night.
It was all about a good Dragon.

A Dragon? said Shiny.
Yes, Shiny, a happy Dragon
that was watching over us.

Yea! Now I know what to get you
for your birthday, Mom. I'll go see
if Handy has one in his store.

Good Morning, Shiny,
said Handy the Octopus.

Handy, Handy, I want to give my Mom
a Dragon for her birthday, but I have a
problem. I don't know what a Dragon is!
Do you have one in your store?

I'm sorry, Shiny. I don't have a Dragon,
but I know just where you can find one.
Are you ready for an adventure?

I'm always ready for an adventure,
Handy! shouted Shiny.

A Dragon is an animal that only lives in stories.

It's not a real animal.

A Dragon's body is shaped like a Snake and is all covered in scales, just like a Fish! It has paws like a Tiger, with claws like an Eagle. And its head is like a Camel!

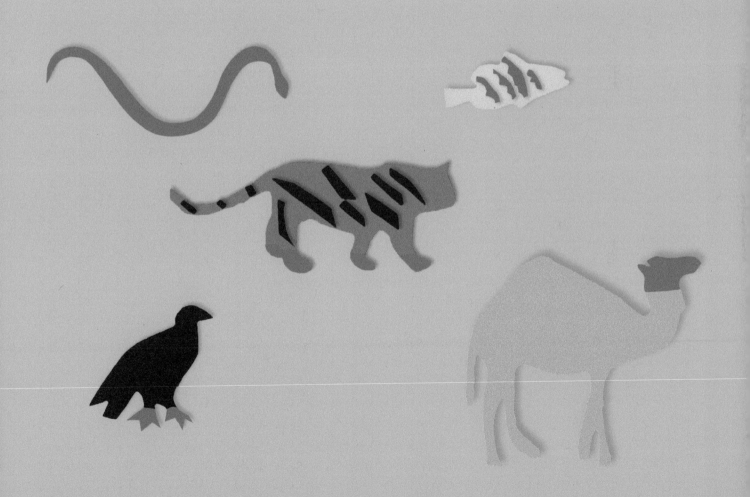

Many great Dragon stories come from China, Shiny.

I am sure you will find a Dragon statue in China for your Mom.

My friend Yo-Yo, the Carp Fish, will help you.
He lives there, on the Yangtze River.

The whole wide world is connected by water, Shiny. That means that you can hop on a wave here in California, and surf your way all over the world.

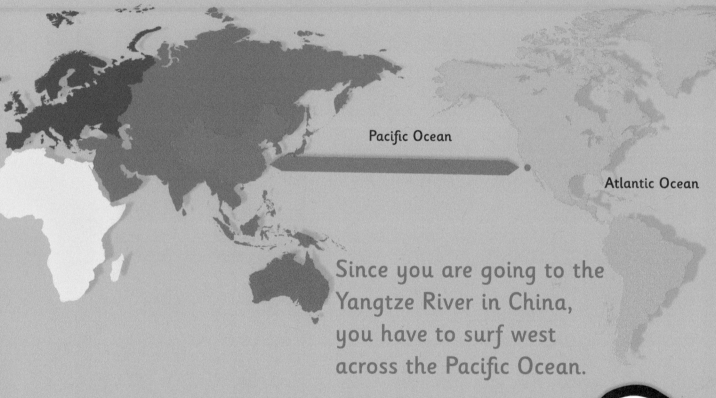

Pacific Ocean

Atlantic Ocean

Since you are going to the Yangtze River in China, you have to surf west across the Pacific Ocean.

A map will show you which way to go. You use a compass to know what direction you are going: north, south, east or west.

We live under the
Santa Monica Pier,

in the city of
Santa Monica,

in the state of California, in the United States of America.

Pacific
Ocean

Atlantic
Ocean

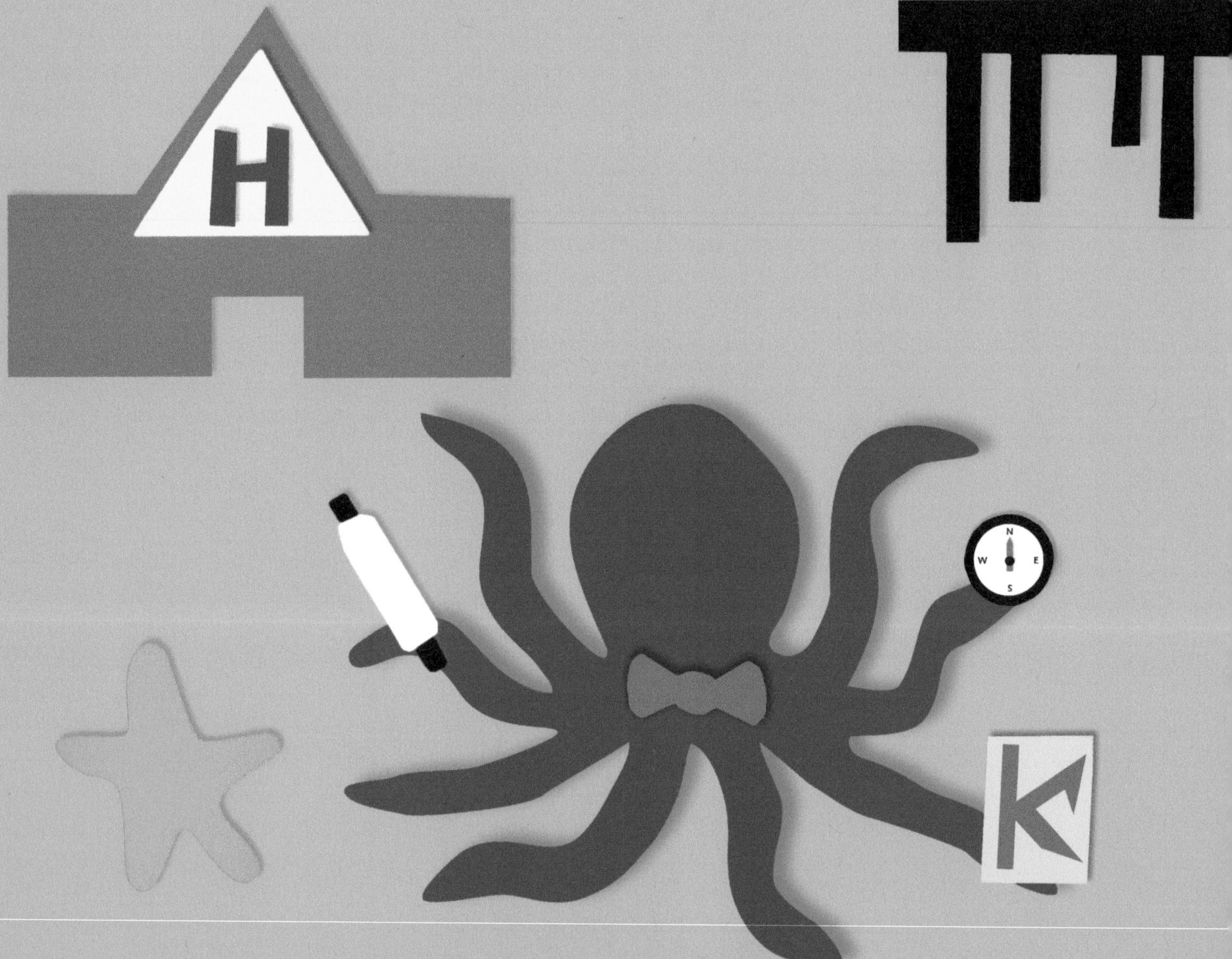
H
N
W
E
S
K

My store doesn't have a Dragon statue, Shiny, but it does have just what you need for your trip to the Yangtze River to find one.

One - Starpack to hold your stuff

Two - Map

Four - Compass

Three - Kelp-O's

Five - Toy Sail Boat

Yo-Yo knows everything about the
Yangtze River. He will help you find
a Dragon statue for your Mom.

I'll send my Seagull Travel
Team to tell Yo-Yo you're coming.

Now, Shiny, LISTEN UP!
See Sulky and Jammer,
the Blowfish over there? You must
NEVER, EVER go near them or
any of their family, BECAUSE
THEY WILL TRY TO EAT YOU!!!!

It's time to start your adventure, Shiny.
Quick, jump on this wave!
I'll tell your Mom you'll be home soon!
Handy shouted.

21

After surfing a very, very, very, long way, about 6,000 miles, Shiny hears a voice calling, Shiny! Shiny! It's Yo-Yo!

You made it to the Yangtze River! I've been waiting for you! Welcome to China!

Oh My Stars! shouted Shiny.
Hi, Yo-Yo!

Just then, a spiky Blowfish came up to them and blocked their way! AHA! shouted the ugly old thing. I have found my lunch!

Oh no you don't, said Yo-Yo, and he slapped the Blowfish away with his strong tail.

That sure was scary, said Shiny.
Yes, said Yo-Yo, but we're safe now.

I know just the place to get your Dragon statue, Shiny. Handy's cousin, Legs, has the best shop on the Yangtze River.

The Yangtze is the longest river in China. It's almost 4,000 miles long. Don't worry, the shop is not too far away. Hop on, Shiny, I'll give you a ride.

Here we are, Shiny.
Jump off!

Yo-Yo! shouted Legs.
I've missed you!

Hi Legs, I've missed you, too.
I've come with my new
friend, Shiny the Sea Star.
He came all the way from
Santa Monica, California,
to find a Dragon statue for
his Mom.

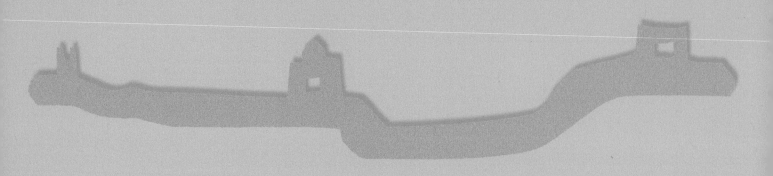

Welcome to China, Shiny. You've come to the right place. My shop has everything, even a picture of our Great Wall.

This Wall was built 2,000 years ago and is really, really long—more than 13,000 miles long; and really, really high—nearly 30 feet high!

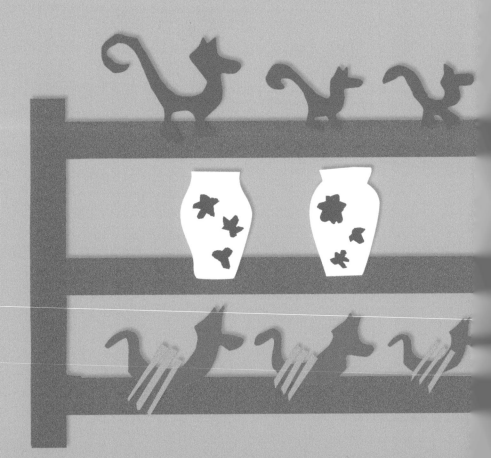

Handy's Seagull Team told me that you are looking for a Dragon statue for your Mom, Shiny. We love Dragons here in China. Our stories tell us that Dragons are brave and strong.

We even tell stories about Dragons making rain.

We build fast Dragon Boats.

We put statues of Dragons on bridges to keep them strong, too.

I see a green Dragon statue, there, on the top shelf. Yo-Yo was right, said Shiny.

Oh My Stars, Legs! You have a boat that looks like a Dragon statue.

Yes, Shiny, that is a toy Dragon Boat, just like the big ones that race during our Dragon Boat Festival. Dragon Boat racing started in China more than 2,000 years ago.

Here, you may have it, and here is the Dragon statue for your Mom. Thank you for coming to visit me.

Thank you! Thank you! Thank you, Legs. I'm ready to go home now, said Shiny.

OK, Shiny, let's leave the Yangtze so you can catch a wave for home.

There's a good wave! Jump off, Shiny! Jump!

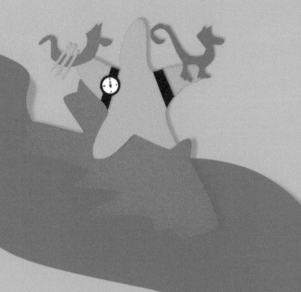

Bye, Shiny! Say
Hi to Handy!
Remember, stay
away from
the Blowfish!

Bye, Yo-Yo! Thank you
for all your help!

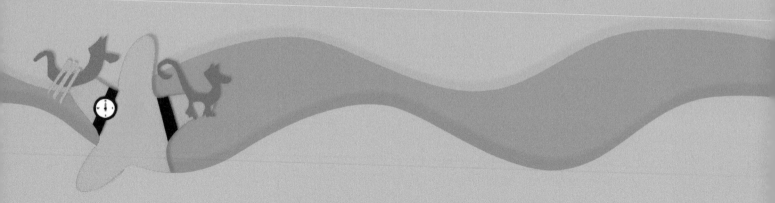

One, Two, Three! Shiny counts as he jumps
on a wave, and surfs the Pacific Ocean to
come home to the Santa Monica Pier.

Mom! Mom! I'm back! I found your
Dragon present! Happy Birthday!
And, I have a Dragon Boat for my
toy boat collection!

Oh, Shiny, this is the best birthday
present EVER!

Thank you! Thank you! Thank you!

Many thanks to María Vélez, from Vélez Design, who turned my Shiny notebooks into shining books.

And to Eleni and William, who were my earliest evaluators and Shiny's first friends.

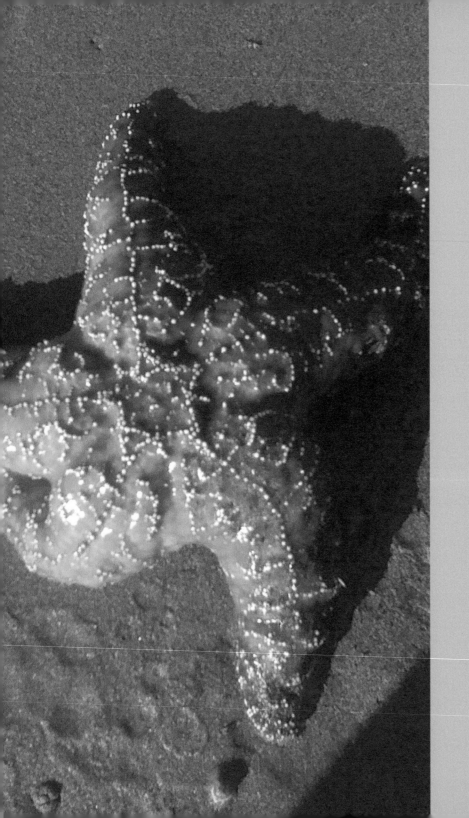

Shiny the Sea Star,
lives under the Santa
Monica Pier, in
Santa Monica,
California.

Cleopatra Bugelas Alexander has been a philanthropy consultant for more than 30 years.

Long committed to education issues, she served on the Board of Evanston/Skokie Elementary School District 65.

She is a graduate of Evanston Township High School and Carleton College.

An avid traveler, she resides in Evanston, Illinois and Santa Monica, California.

Mom! Mom!
Did you know that we can be friends
with the WHOLE WORLD, because we
are all connected by water? I can surf
across the water and stop at rivers and
make new friends EVERYWHERE!

Yes, Shiny. You have learned an
important lesson. We all share
the same water and we all can,
and should, be friends.

Which river will you visit next?

N

ARCTIC OCEAN

NORTH
AMERICA

NORTH
ATLANTIC
OCEAN

EUROPE

Baltic
Sea

Volga

Danube

Black
Sea

Caspian
Sea

ASIA

Mediterranean Sea

Mississippi

Yangtze

AFRICA

Ganges

PACIFIC
OCEAN

Caribbean
Sea

Red Sea

Nile

Amazon

PACIFIC
OCEAN

SOUTH
AMERICA

INDIAN
OCEAN

SOUTH
ATLANTIC
OCEAN

AUSTRALIA

Murray-Darling

| 0 | 1000 | 2000 Km |
| 0 | 500 | 1000 Miles |

SOUTHERN OCEAN